I LOVE YOU, DADDY!

BY EDIE EVANS
ILLUSTRATED BY RUSTY FLETCHER

For my Dad, Sherman Levin

—E.E.

A GOLDEN BOOK • NEW YORK
Golden Books Publishing Company, Inc., New York, New York 10106

We'd be happy to answer your questions and hear your comments. Please call us toll free at 1-888-READ-2-ME (1-888-732-3263). Hours: 8 AM–8 PM EST, weekdays. US and Canada only.

Daddy, I love you,
and I want you to know,
I have a great time
wherever we go.

At the carwash we pretend we're deep in the sea, and the brushes are fish waving their fins at me.

Camping is my favorite
summer event.
We sleep in the woods—
I help pitch the tent!

We plant seeds out back
in neat, straight rows,
and then water them
with the garden hose.

Going to the petting zoo
is always lots of fun.
We feed goats, pigs, and sheep
out in the bright, warm sun.

When snow covers the ground
and the hills are all white,
we sled and make snowballs
from morning to night.

At the neighborhood park
we jump, swing, and play.
Soon the sun sets.
Have we been here all day?

I love you, Daddy,
for all that we do.
In a contest for best dad,
the winner is you!